Cally Hart
and the
Fairy
Sparks

◆ FriesenPress

One Printers Way
Altona, MB R0G 0B0
Canada

www.friesenpress.com

Books may be purchased by contacting the author at:
www.deannakweensauthor.com

Graphic artist of front cover, inside covers, chapters, map and back cover: Janice Blaine

Editors: Michelle Superle and Larissa D'Silva

ISBN
978-1-03-911905-5 (Hardcover)
978-1-03-911904-8 (Paperback)
978-1-03-911906-2 (eBook)

1. JUVENILE FICTION, FANTASY & MAGIC

Distributed to the trade by The Ingram Book Company

Cally Hart
and the
Fairy
Sparks

DeAnna Kweens

INTRODUCTION

Dear friends,

This book is dedicated to all the kids of the world, no matter what age you count in numbers. Please know that your unique sensitivities are gifts to this world. You are teaching the world how to love more and to choose love over and over again.

And so, I want to reintroduce you to the loving helpers you have along the way: the fairies, angels, unicorns, dragons, and many other mystical light beings who are here with you right now. You know them already; they are a part of you.

As you read this book, notice how you feel during this adventure. I hope you know how much love surrounds you at every moment. And that when you feel different, I hope you know that means that you're exactly where you need to be.

Enjoy your journey and may your reconnection to the divine come back to you with every turn of these pages.

Sending all the unlimited love in the universe to you, my friend!

DeAnna

Fairyland

CHAPTER 1

Cally

I felt sleepy after school like I always did after being around a lot of people, but as soon as I closed my eyes, I heard a faint whisper in my ear.

"Notice the sparks," the voice said.

I opened my eyes and saw a bright purple spark nestled on the plastic stars on my bedroom ceiling. It grew as I focused on it. Within seconds, the spark was surrounded by a purple glow that seemed to be moving. I blinked to make sure it was real. It disappeared.

Suddenly, I felt a strong wind move against my hair.

"What's that?" I said aloud. All at once, I felt energized and my hands were vibrating.

Then a strong gust of wind from nowhere started swirling in the middle of my room, and all the plastic stars fell off the ceiling. They swirled around me until they all landed in the same order on my bed as they had been on the ceiling.

I blinked again, trying to figure out what was going on.

"Is this a dream?" I asked my dog, Max, who was lying beside me as usual. He'd barely left my side since my dad left last year. It all happened so quickly, and Dad didn't even say goodbye.

Max looked at me with his warm brown eyes and tucked his coarse black nose near my thigh.

All of a sudden, my tablet started playing energetic dance music. It was so loud we both jumped.

As I scrambled to turn it off, the gust of wind floated past my hair again, causing goose-bumps on my neck.

When I looked for where the wind was coming from, the music turned off.

Then I realized Max was gone.

"Can you be quieter in there?" my mom said in her strong Irish accent from the laundry room beside me. "I don't want your brother to wake from his nap, or he'll be up all night."

"Sorry, Mom!" I said. If there was anything I *didn't* want, it was to add to Mom's problems. She had so many things to do. I just wanted her to be happy again—her old self.

As I reached for my tablet again, the purple glowing light was now beside it. I reached out to touch the glow, but just as my fingertips felt warmth, the light moved slowly across my room until it disappeared through my bedroom door.

I was curious about the glow, so I grabbed my purple jacket and followed it.

The light was moving quickly down the stairs and into the living room. I was staring at it so hard that I didn't see the beanbag toy on the steps. I fell down the stairs into Max's doggie bed, taking in a mouthful of golden retriever hair.

"Cally, what happened? Are you all right?" Mom rushed over to help me up as I picked the hair out of my mouth.

"I'm so tired of Wes's toys lying around everywhere. I could have broken my leg!" I rubbed my knee.

"I'm sorry, lass, I haven't had time to pick them up. Why are you being so dramatic? And why were you running down the stairs in the first place?" Mom looked at me straight in the eyes, and I felt terrible. Here I was making her feel worse, when all I wanted was to make her feel better. The toys didn't really matter. I should pick them up myself, to help Mom. I *would*, as soon as I figured out what was going on with the purple spark.

"It was nothing, sorry. I was just going to take Max for a walk," I said, gaining back my balance and looking away from her serious stare. If only I could make her happy.

"Good idea, you should enjoy the fall weather before it gets cold again. Just make sure you're back in time for supper."

She walked to the kitchen. I just wanted her to turn around and pick me up, like she did when I was five and we used to go on bike rides around the neighbourhood with my dad. She was different then, laughing and racing us until we got home.

"Go, Cally, go!" she always yelled as we reached our driveway.

I would giggle as she slowed down just enough for me to win.

"Cally, my wee lass, you won!" She'd scoop me up in her arms, and we'd both laugh as she tickled me uncontrollably.

But ever since my dad left last year, she'd been too busy to play or chat.

I pushed the thought out of my mind and looked around to find the spark. I couldn't see it, but I could hear Max jumping with excitement in the living room. When I got there he was circling around the spark playfully, just like he did when he was chasing a soccer ball.

The spark moved toward the front door. Max and I followed.

CHAPTER 2
Jackson

I was playing with my new Star Wars Lego set in my room when I felt her coming down the sidewalk. It's hard to explain how I can feel her presence, but there's something about Cally Hart. She's always so gentle and scattered. It's like she's playing with magical creatures in her head, even though she's eleven years old.

I looked out my bedroom window, and sure enough, it was Cally and her dog, Max, hurrying down the street.

By the time I got to them, Cally stood looking at the biggest oak tree in the park.

Her frizzy red curls were all over the place, and she seemed to be in her own little world.

"Hey, Cally! What's going on?" I tried to catch my breath.

"Oh, hi, Jackson! This is going to sound crazy, but I think I was led to this exact spot by . . ." She started circling the tree. Max followed her.

"By what, Cally?" I said loudly. Sometimes she drove me crazy.

She stopped in front of the tree and pointed to it. When she finally looked at me, she said, "I saw a purple spark of light in my room. I think it wanted me to come here."

It's my job to bring Cally back to reality when she's daydreaming or setting off on what she thinks will be a wonderful adventure. Somebody has to do it. She can't look after herself. I mean, really—she even spaces out in mid-conversation sometimes! And who knows what kind of trouble Cally could get into this time.

Cally looked at me with her hazel-brown eyes shining against her caramel skin. One of the stars from her bedroom ceiling was stuck in her curly red hair. Who else but Cally would have stars in her hair?

"What?" Cally asked.

"You have a star stuck in your hair." Did this girl ever look in a mirror?

"I don't care! I'm following this thing that I've been trying to figure out for the last half an hour," she said.

"Okay, Cally. What thing?" I asked, fiddling with my glasses.

"This isn't my imagination, Jackson. This bright purple light started glowing in my room. Then some sort of wind blew the stars off my ceiling. It seemed like the spark was trying to get me to follow it. So I did."

I was about to roll my eyes and then decided to play along. This was obviously important to her. "Where is it now?"

"It disappeared. But . . . can you hear that? There's some sort of song in the wind," she said, looking back at the tree and then watching Max wag his tail. "I think Max can hear it, too."

"What are you talking about? I don't hear anything. Besides, what does that have to do with the spark?"

"I have no idea. But it must have led us here for a reason!" She clapped her hands like she always does when she's excited.

I stepped closer to the tree, and a swirl of leaves danced up around my feet. Then I heard the song from the wind.

There is magic everywhere
If only you allow yourself to see
There are sparks in everything

*As we are present wherever we
can give you gifts to receive
Like the hollow of this tree
Like the slide ride that leads you
to our sacred place
A place of wonder and magic
A place of elemental harmony
So welcome to our land
Welcome to our home
We are excited to welcome
you here
As you will change and grow
Welcome, welcome, welcome
To the land of the sparks, the
land of the fairies.*

When the song ended, the tree started to move.

CHAPTER 3
Cally

The moving oak tree turned into the tallest man I'd ever seen. He was so tall that it took me a while to see his face at the top of the tree. The branches of the tree were his arms, and the bottom roots of the tree were like his feet. He stretched his roots as his mouth formed a big sigh, making the ground around my feet vibrate.

Jackson and I looked at each other and then back at the tree. Just being near the tree man sent a strong wave of energy through my feet and legs. In that moment, my legs felt ready to dance. I could hardly stop myself.

Jackson's small mouth hung open. This wasn't something you saw every day, and routine was his middle name.

"Are you okay, Jackson?" I nudged his broad shoulder gently. It was sort of funny to see his face turn as white as a ghost, but I felt bad for him, too. He never liked surprises after his mom passed away.

He just stood there with his straight brown hair swept back off his forehead like it always was. He pushed it back over and over all day to calm himself. Then he adjusted the square glasses that hid his distinct blueish-green eyes and light freckles. He always fiddled with his glasses when he was nervous.

Typical Jackson—so quiet when things are unexplainable.

This look of shock on his face reminded me of the time I told him that I thought Max could read our thoughts. He was shocked at first, but he eventually got used to the idea. Now I sometimes think he's talking to Max through his thoughts.

I could feel Jackson thinking to me now, *Is this is for real*?

I said aloud, "I think so."

The tree man mesmerized me. Its branches seemed like they were always supposed to move that way. It looked so natural.

"Welcome, my friends. My name is the Green Man."

I laughed out of excitement, but Jackson just kept staring at the tree.

"I'm Cally!" I said, which sent a wave of happiness through me.

In that moment, I realized I'd seen him before. I remembered one evening when I was four years old, lying next to my mom in her bed.

"What would you like me to read to you tonight, my wee lass?" She was smiling. She always smiled back then.

"How about this one?" I asked, pointing to a big picture book called *Auras from the Trees*.

"Oh, that's a classic!" Mom's green eyes sparkled like the green of the trees.

The warm and striking face I was looking up at now was the same one that had decorated the book's cover.

After I read that book, I started looking for him everywhere, especially the many trees in our yard. I finally saw him a few months later when my volleyball landed by an old spruce tree near the schoolyard fence. For one quick instant, I saw a man's smiling face looking back at me from the tree. His mossy-green eyes winked at me as I closed mine quickly to make sure he was real.

"I know you," he said now. The Green Man's wise eyes winked at me. I saw dark brown tree rings around them as he winked again.

"I wondered whether I'd ever see you again," I said, stepping closer to him and reaching my hands towards the tree without realizing it.

"I only pop up when you need me." The Green Man winked at me again.

"Since I last saw you, sometimes I think of you and feel your tree roots under my feet." I noticed his roots sparkle.

"Why do you think that happens?" He smiled.

The answer came to me quickly.

"When I feel your roots under my feet I feel better, like they're helping to bring me into the moment. Sort of . . . back to myself." I smiled back at him.

"Yes, that's it," he agreed. "And who have you brought with you?"

"This is my friend Jackson and my dog, Max." Jackson was so busy looking at the tree and how it was so alive and human-like that he didn't look up. Max let out one of his unique barks.

"Welcome, Max and Jackson. I had a feeling you were coming today." The Green Man stretched one of his roots. "What brought you here this time?" He looked at me.

What did he mean, *this time*? Had I been here before? How could I forget such a thing?

"I saw a spark in my room, and it led us here. But I'm not sure why."

"I know why. But sometimes it's better to experience things rather than explain. Are you up for an adventure? Do you want to learn?" the Green Man asked, gently nudging me with one of his branches.

"Yes!" I shouted. This time I let myself dance.

Max got so excited that his tongue dropped out his mouth, and his eyes sparkled with glee.

But Jackson was biting his nails. "Is this safe? It seems too good to be true."

"Trust me, Jackson, we'll be fine." I hugged him before I remembered that he hated being touched.

But he stepped closer and hugged me back. I could feel my heart skip a beat and sing at the same time as we both shouted, "Yes!"

With one smooth motion, the Green Man extended his strong roots down through the ground in front of us, opening up the earth.

CHAPTER 4
Jackson

I couldn't believe this. Was I really going to let Cally drag me along on a moving tree root attached to a tree calling himself the Green Man? I was supposed to be keeping Cally *safe*! Why do I always follow her?

My dad had been telling me that I needed to be more adventurous. I used to be. I can remember that when I was younger, I always followed the butterflies fluttering around the flowers in our backyard. I ran after them as they flew to their next flower petal—spending hours without even realizing it.

I loved those butterflies. I wished I had their wings. I always wanted to fly.

But it hasn't been the same since Mom passed. I remember the moment my dad sat next to me and my mom on the couch and said very lightly, "Jackson . . ." I knew right away something was up as he said, "Mommy is sick."

My heart had dropped into my stomach. I couldn't believe it was real. All I could do was grab both of their hands as we sat there for a long time.

Every day after that I asked the butterflies in the garden to make her better. But a few months later, a rainbow butterfly with electric-sapphire, pink, orange, violet, and yellow specks landed on my palm. It flew away as soon as my dad appeared with puffy eyes, and then I knew—my most favourite person in the whole world was gone. After that, I didn't even want to go outside.

"Earth to Jackson, are you seeing this?!" Cally's voice boomed in my ear.

She pointed at the roots lighting up beneath us. I tried to feel the tree's root with my hand to see if it was real as I walked along. It felt like any other tree. But the strange thing was that when I touched the root, it made me feel lighter.

"It's like the Green Man knows where we're stepping." Cally touched the root beside me. The root lit up with a soft purple light beneath her palm. Suddenly, all the tree roots started to move towards the top of the tree like an escalator.

"It feels like we're floating on a cloud!" Cally held onto the roots for support and smiled so big I thought her face was going to explode.

"Wake me up from this anytime," I said back, knowing it sounded more sarcastic than I meant it. I just felt unsteady and needed to make sense of it all.

As we neared the top of the old tree, I could tell Cally was happy. Her dimples glowed as she sat down on the roots and held on.

Max was having the time of his life. His mouth was all the way open with his big gooey tongue sticking out just like when he was playing fetch.

As the roots came to a stop, I noticed something that looked like a bird hole almost hidden behind a bunch of intertwined roots. Before I could examine it more, the roots moved apart automatically. I froze, clutching at the branch. This was crazy! Where was this weird tree taking us? My stomach started to churn like it always does when I'm scared.

Max barked and jumped into the hole without hesitation. Cally followed him, but she turned around to look at me before entering. I remembered that she's scared of heights.

Cally was turning pale as she looked down at me, so I jumped up and stood beside her. My stomach felt better right away.

Cally looked at me with certainty in her eyes. "We can do this, Jackson!"

"Or we can turn back," I said to her, remembering my mission to keep her safe. "This is kind of crazy. There's no harm in just turning around and going home."

She looked at me and said, as she fiddled with her tangled curls, "No. I'm ready. I just shouldn't have looked down. I need to do this. I need to find out why we're here!"

I realized she was about to cry. Her hands were shaking. Suddenly, keeping her safe seemed like a different job than I'd thought at first.

"The Green Man seems like a pretty cool tree," I said, trying to put her at ease.

"I AM PRETTY COOL." The tree roots vibrated with these words as the Green Man's voice emerged around us. "It's probably because I am so connected to the deep earth. Trees are cool like that," he said after a moment.

I smiled, and Cally giggled. Her smiley dimples returned.

Then the landing started to move further inside, towards the Green Man's heart. A deeper opening appeared, and Max led the way again.

It was times like these that I loved having Max around. He was braver than Cally and me.

I think most animals are. They have a natural way of being so wise.

I remembered the day Cally got Max. She ran into my bedroom huffing and puffing. She'd obviously run all the way over to my house. "Jackson, come downstairs right now!" she shouted.

I put down my favourite dinosaur book, *Calls from the Earth*.

"Why?" I looked back at her, frustrated by the interruption.

"Just come and see." Cally started to walk out my bedroom door.

"You always do this, Cally!" I could feel my face starting to get red. "I don't feel like following you around today."

"Ever since you lost your mom, you hardly ever leave your room." Cally looked down. "I miss you, Jackson."

"That's not true. I just liking being home," I replied.

"This surprise is worth it, trust me." She smiled lightly and looked at me again.

"I don't feel like it, Cally," I said, picking my book up again.

She grabbed the book from my hands and ran downstairs. I reluctantly followed, but then I saw my dad patting a six-week-old puppy with a soft yellow fur coat, innocent brown eyes, and small droopy ears.

"Golden retrievers were your mom's favourite," my dad said to me as I got closer. Tears collected in his rich brown eyes. "She would have loved having a dog like this."

I tried to smile at Dad as he grew quiet.

"I named him Max! That's short for Maximus Prime from *Transformers*." Cally smiled bigger than I knew she could.

Max's gleeful bark snapped me back to the present. He appeared to be going down a slide in the tree. Cally jumped and clapped in front of me as the roots inside the hole took us on a ride.

Now, I'd been to Disneyland, but I'd never experienced anything like this before. This tree slide moved smoothly through the inside of the tree. Every area we passed lit up with white golden light as we went by. There seemed to be many tunnels and slides around us, leading in all different directions.

To my right, a soft white slide glistened. White haloed figures danced upon it. As we passed the slide, the figures looked at me. Some of them hopped behind me on our slide, and I saw a glimpse of a rainbow butterfly that made me think of my mom. Before I could see it again, a ghostlike mermaid and unicorn ran around my head in mid-air. I reached out to touch them, but they hopped back onto their slide, which was moving away from ours.

To my left, a turquoise-blue tunnel lit up with bright blue sparkles that looked like shiny gemstones with sharp edges. The tunnel was very bright but completely quiet.

Then I saw a golden-plated opening above us. It was another tunnel. The entrance was guarded by three black cats who stared at me as a big dip in our slide led us deeper into the earth.

"I wonder where all these slides go," Cally said as we moved past them.

"I hope we get to come back to explore them," I said, surprising myself. That was strange. I didn't want to get right back home like I usually did. "I want to see where they lead to!"

"All in perfect timing." The Green Man's voice echoed throughout the hollow of the tree.

Then the Green Man started to sing the song we'd heard before. The louder it got, the more adventurous I felt. Riding the slide suddenly felt like flying. Then many different voices joined in—it was like a choir of voices was welcoming us.

More multicoloured sparks of light than I could ever count surrounded us, filling up the slide as we slid to the bottom of the tree. The singing faded away.

Then the tree echoed with the Green Man's next words, "Welcome to Fairyland!"

CHAPTER 5
Cally

As I stepped off the Green Man's thick roots, it was like jumping into a bubble of instant happiness.

There was so much to see. Multiple sparks of coloured light surrounded me. Rich and soft greens, blues, pinks, yellows, oranges, and reds. As I looked at the sparks more closely, the colours became so clear, so vivid. They cocooned me. I was in a swirl of magic.

"This is amazing!" I said aloud. My arms felt like soaring.

The shimmering creatures radiated an infectious joyfulness and happiness. Their endearing smiles made me feel safe and loved instantly—just like I used to feel all the time with my mom. I wished she could see this.

"Hello to you all!" my voice squeaked with excitement.

"Hi, Cally! Welcome, welcome, welcome!" small voices replied in unison.

Some of them were covered in flowers—orchids, roses, snapdragons, and many more I didn't even know the names of. Some looked like trees. Some were flying in mid-air, and others were walking on the ground. Some looked like reflections in water. They seemed to get clearer and happier as I moved my hands closer to them. They were excited to see me and to show me who they were.

When I reached out my hands and touched the beings, soft tingles travelled through my fingertips. Gentle giggles came from the sparks as some of them jumped on my arm and bounced up and down. With every bounce their lights twinkled brighter. Warmth filled up my heart.

I squealed as I felt something bouncing near my right elbow. A bright lime-green spark appeared as I looked closer.

A Celtic song came from the spark:

> *Oh, Cally girl, the fairies are*
> *calling you*
> *With every blink you take*
> *Our magic is here for you.*

A violin chord carried the melody as the spark swayed with the music.

When the music drifted away, the spark turned into a little green childlike person, dancing and singing loudly, "*Oh, Cally girl, the fairies are calling you.*"

He stood the height of a quarter. His hair was spiky and green. His tiny feet were the size of my freckles, and they sent out green sparkly pixie dust as he enthusiastically tap danced along my hand.

"You're a beautiful dancer!" I smiled at him.

"Oh, my. Thanks, Cally!" The green fairy flipped up into the air and onto the ground as all the other sparks on my arms flew back into the air around me.

"Can I call you Celtic Thunder?" I asked as he settled on my palm.

He smiled kindly and blew a small kiss towards me. Deep green light danced around his feet.

Then I noticed a huge rock circle further in the land on my left, similar to one I'd seen in pictures of Stonehenge in England. To my right, I saw tree houses that encompassed a whole forest.

So many different plants and different types of little and life-size beings lived beyond here in this magical forest with waterfalls, meadows, lakes, and mountains. We'd landed in a small area, but the land seemed to go on further than I could see. Everything was so bright, so green and alive.

"There's got to be millions of beings here." I looked at Jackson.

He adjusted his glasses and pointed. "Are those clouds really doing what I think?"

As I looked up to the bright blue sky, I could see the clouds form into shapes of more fairies. One cloud fairy looked like she was diving into a pool. Another was holding a dandelion with the fluff floating away into the wind.

"I haven't dreamt of magical places like this since I was younger," Jackson said.

"Well, maybe it's time to believe again." I stepped closer to him, and the area around his head started to glow a dark blue colour.

"It's safe here," I said confidently back to him. The blue colour faded around his head. Silence filled the space between us.

I felt a quick breeze around my hand.

"Cally, what's that moving light on your hand?!" Jackson flicked my hand, and Celtic Thunder toppled over.

"Hey!" Celtic Thunder's light shone brighter as he stood up again.

"You're going to hurt him!" I cocooned Celtic Thunder with my other hand.

"What are you talking about? What *him*?" Jackson stared at my cupped hands.

"Didn't you see them when you looked closer at the lights on our way into Fairyland?"

He slouched his shoulders. "No."

"That's weird, I did."

I heard Celtic Thunder speak from my palm, "He doesn't see me the way that you do because he's not meant to at this time."

Then the small green fairy jumped back near my elbow as a small lime-coloured elf appeared from behind a tall red maple tree. He had the cutest leafy outfit and pointy ears.

He was half the size of Jackson, with a long face and rounded chin.

Max stood up and barked at the elf as if saying hello.

Jackson didn't say anything as he leaned down to pat Max. Then he asked, "How do you know the elf?"

A certainty came over me. "I think Max has been here before." I smiled gently, looking down at Max.

"Yeah! I think you're right! I bet Max has been to a lot of different tunnels and slides. He seemed really familiar with the tree slide. He jumped on it without hesitation and knew exactly where we were going."

I clapped my hands with excitement. Jackson seemed to relax for a moment. Then he asked, "Where do you think all those tunnels and slides lead to?"

The green Celtic Thunder fairy hopped back on my arm from the ground and started dancing again. In that moment I knew in my heart and said aloud, "There must be similar lands like this one where magical beings live. Ever since we arrived I've been feeling more certain about things. I just know them more here than back home—it's hard to explain." I was surprised at my own words.

As soon as I finished talking, the light that I had seen go into the park tree started to expand into multiple colours.

As the light expanded even more, a human-like figure with wings appeared. She gently touched down on the ground with green light pooling around her feet. She had a kind smile as she appeared. She stood about half my size. Her emerald-green eyes landed on me as her beautiful white curly locks of hair surrounded her dark brown face. Light followed just behind her, and she left a trail of yellow tulips in her path. She had transparent purple dragonfly wings that moved with every breath she took.

Goosebumps travelled up my arms, and a warm feeling entered my heart. I was overcome by her presence, her beauty, her perfection. I almost felt like I was going to cry.

"Hi, Cally, I've been waiting for you," she said in a gentle voice as she sent this wave of purple energy towards my heart. "I'm glad you finally followed me. It took a lot of movement in your room to get you to listen." Her green eyes sparkled.

Max automatically curled up to her. His tongue was sticking out in glee.

I felt like I already knew her. But that was impossible.

"It's nice to see you again, Max. I missed your warm hugs." She looked at him as she floated a bit off the ground.

"How do you know Max and me?" I asked shyly.

"Well, you asked for me before you came into this life, just like many people do. I'm not the first fairy who's been with you in this one either," she said.

"Who else is there?!" I asked excitedly. I was definitely curious.

The purple fairy smiled and said, "We'll connect with some of them very soon."

"So, what do I call you?" I asked.

"What would you like to call me?" She started to swing lightly back and forth in front of me.

Out of nowhere, a picture of the Greek goddess Athena that I studied in English class popped into my head.

Before I could say it aloud, she enthusiastically said, "Yes, Athena is my name!"

How could she know what I was thinking? Mom really needed to see this. I knew it would make her happier.

I took a deep breath in and asked, "So, we've met before?"

Jackson interrupted me, seeming to feel left out. "I'm Jackson. Cally's best friend."

"I know, you've been friends since you were three. We all used to play together in your backyard."

"What? But how?" I asked.

"The answer is already inside of you," Athena said, nearly singing her words.

"But...what about..." I mumbled, bewildered.

"Don't worry. The answers will come more easily as you let yourself listen and receive," she said softly. "For now, let's go to the fairy pond. There's lots to see while you're here. Soon you'll stop believing, and that's a whole other story."

Then a massive white spark of light beamed down from the sky. The light got brighter, and swirls of blue surrounded it as a strong mystical horse with a sparkling horn emerged from the light to land on the ground in front of us.

It felt just as natural to get on the magical unicorn as it did to snuggle up under a soft quilt that my grandpa gave me before he passed away. Jackson surprised me by being the first to move onto the wing the unicorn extended out to us. Max and I followed, with Athena flying beside us.

CHAPTER 6
Jackson

The unicorn soared up into the sky. My hands were sweaty and trembling by the time we reached the fluffy clouds. Were we safe? I watched Cally's face. She was happier than I'd seen her since her dad left.

She looked at me calmly and said, "You can do this."

My hands shook as I looked down. From the air, the land seemed to go on forever. There were fairies like Athena everywhere, flying in the air, walking on the ground, lying in the trees, and floating on the water. Everywhere! They were big and small and many different ages. Then I noticed a variety of mystical creatures roaming the land below.

I gripped on tighter to the unicorn, seeing more elves and what looked like gnomes and dwarves from the books I had read when my mom was sick.

When I realized we had almost reached the centre of this land, I started to relax a bit. Cally was giggling with excitement. Then a jolly, round face appeared in the sky. It was talking to a large willow tree on the ground below.

Everything in the land seemed to revolve around the willow tree itself. I felt warmth radiating from the tree, a connection to the earth.

I blinked. *Was this real?*

"That's Mother Earth and Father Sky," said a happy voice. It sounded like my own voice inside my head.

The more I saw, the more I believed. The more I believed, the more vivid everything got.

A warm, safe, loving energy lit up in my heart. It had been such a long time since I'd felt so good.

Max loved this place, too. He was drooling and overjoyed. His tongue stuck out, and he looked as if he were floating.

There was a warm energy beside me, too. It was coming from Cally. She seemed more energetic than before, all excited with sparkles filling up her brown eyes.

"I'm on top of the world!" she shouted gleefully.

I was happy for her. She had told me once that even with people around her, she felt alone.

I totally understood that feeling. Ever since my mom died, my dad has been so sad, and my brother has been so angry. I wished we spent more time together.

A familiar sadness dropped into my stomach as it always did when I thought about my mom. But then the unicorn looked back at me for a moment, and somehow I felt better and more secure. Like I was meant to be here, wishing I could bring this feeling home with me.

Before I could look below at the land again, Athena reappeared. Flying beside me, she smiled and pointed down.

There were gnomes dancing around a fire while fairies sang songs that echoed through the land. Birds chirped so loud that I could even hear them high up in the sky. Some of the fairies joined them, flying and singing with the birds. Plants in a meadow talked to one another. The sun was shining so brightly that it was as if it was singing love for the land.

Cally couldn't stop smiling.

"Are we in a dream, Jackson?" Cally looked at me.

"I've been asking myself the same thing for the last few minutes." We laughed together.

"I'm so happy you followed that spark!" I said.

"I'm glad you finally got some fairy giggles," Athena piped in. A stream of light and yellow tulips trailed behind her.

I looked at them, and we all chuckled in mid-air together.

CHAPTER 7
Cally

When Athena and the unicorn started to descend, the light around the unicorn faded into a soft blue the closer we got to the ground.

We landed on a beautiful mossy cliff that overlooked a waterfall cascading down into a sparkling lagoon. As we all got off the unicorn, my energy was floating. Max started dancing around excitedly. I joined him, and then Athena came, too. We formed a dance circle.

"Come and dance with us, Jackson!" I motioned to him.

"You know I'm not a great dancer." Jackson fixed his glasses and turned away to look at the lagoon below.

"Everyone can dance!" I yelled back, shuffling my feet to show him it didn't have to be perfect.

Max left the circle to nudge Jackson's legs with his yellow paw.

"Fine." Jackson kicked a stone on his way to join in the fun.

The bubble of silliness and lightness we were creating made me feel like I used to when Jackson and I were really little. Suddenly, I remembered a time Jackson and I were playing in his backyard when we were about four years old.

We were running and laughing as we chased a yellow light until it darted into Jackson's tree house. The vision faded away as I saw the look on Jackson's face. He was so alive!

He shouted, "Hey, it feels good to move. I like this place!"

The unicorn circled around us once more before she flew away. Her light beamed brighter as she floated up to the sky and into the wispy clouds. As the light disappeared, Athena landed on the ground beside us, and motioned for us to follow her. Her purple glow surrounded all of us as her wings fluttered softly.

She took us to an opening under a holly tree where she held back a mesh curtain that was actually made of grass. It was dark at first, and Jackson hesitated. He was afraid of the dark. I was the only person who knew he still slept with a night light because sometimes he felt things around him that he couldn't explain.

"There's nothing to fear, it will light up in a second. It will be worth it, I promise." Athena touched Jackson's shoulder.

"How did you know I was afraid?" Jackson asked Athena, fidgeting with his shirt collar.

"I could feel your thoughts as I moved back the curtain. All you need to do is just trust yourself, Jackson," Athena said confidently.

Max and I jumped into the opening. Jackson followed.

In front of us was the lagoon we had seen earlier.

"Welcome to your fairy-team pond," Athena said, opening her arms wide.

The water in the lagoon smiled at me. It was the most beautiful sparkling turquoise water I'd ever seen. Its smile was infectious, so I smiled back without realizing it. Then I saw my face smile back at me in the reflection.

"Cally, you have a lot of water fairies that can help you. They're part of your divine team, a diverse group of many magical beings that support you and love you unconditionally, no matter what. And that's just the water fairies! There are so many others," Athena said as she walked beside me.

"Oh, wow! That must be because I've always loved water. My parents used to tell me that I was like a fish every time we went swimming in the summer," I said happily.

Athena smiled and walked towards Max and Jackson, who were now on the other side of the waterfall.

All of a sudden a blue speck of light quickly floated over the water.

The blue speck expanded until white-and-gold light glistened around it in the air. I reached for the blue light as it moved into the sandy beach near the water. My fingertips tingled with goosebumps that somehow warmed me. Then, as suddenly as it had appeared, the blue light vanished into the sand.

"Hey! Don't go! What's your name?" I asked.

Instantly, I saw "Sandy" written in the light brown sand below my feet. The letters glistened in gold and blue.

"Cool." I smiled.

The sand swirled up and formed into a fairy with brown wings that somehow looked like a tiny little girl—even though she had no face.

She moved to the water, and before I could blink, she splashed me.

I laughed, and she moved back to the sand out of sight.

"This is fun, Sandy! Why do you keep disappearing?" I asked, running after her.

The words "Because I can" appeared before my feet in the sand.

"That's her way of saying hi—she likes to connect with your emotions," said a voice behind my ear.

I turned to look, but nothing was there.

"I'm up here, Cally!" said the voice.

I looked above me and saw a three-foot-tall boy fairy with orange wings and a pink body. Orange-and-pink light glowed around him.

"Sandy and I have been waiting for you to visit!" He swirled and twisted through the sky, then touched on the lagoon before making his way to my feet on the ground.

I knelt down to his height and smiled so big at him. "Is that so? Why?"

"Cally, we've been watching over you since you were a baby. We are part of your fairy guardian team." He smiled.

"What can I call you?" I asked as he twisted in the air.

"Whatever you'd like—just trust your heart," he said as he sent an orange light into my head. I knew in that moment that I wanted to call him Skye.

Suddenly, sand flew up towards my face, and I saw the words, "It's okay to feel the way you do about your mom," written by my shoes.

My shoulders felt heavy for an instant.

"We want you to shake off that heaviness . . . try this." Skye jumped up and down, and shook his body in front of me.

I started copying his movements "That's it—let that heaviness move through you and into the ground." After a while, I felt better.

Skye smiled and flew into the sky, saying, "Visit us anytime, here or in your world. Just think or call our names, and we'll be there for you!"

Then he was gone.

CHAPTER 8
Jackson

"Why haven't I met any of my fairies yet?" I asked Athena while we were walking along the lagoon.

"You have! Do you remember having an imaginary friend when you were younger?" Athena glowed as she asked.

"Hhhhmmm . . . I remember my parents joked about me insisting on having an extra place at the table until I was five. They said I called him Teddy. But I don't remember that," I said.

"He's one of your fairies, Jackson," Athena said with a look of sadness on her face. She was quiet for a while.

"Where did he go?" I finally asked.

"Sometimes when children ask us not to be around anymore or not to play with them . . . well, they stop seeing us. Eventually, the children even stop believing in us." Athena paused and then said, "By the time they become adults, most have forgotten we exist." Her wings dropped down by her side.

I remembered all the times I'd doubted Cally's talk about magical creatures.

"We're always here. Humans just let the world talk them into not believing anymore as they get older. So the world has given us a bad name. But we just want to help you! That's what we're here to do."

"Help? What kind of help?" I asked, secretly hoping Athena could bring my mother back to me.

"If people knew what walked or flew beside them," Athena said, her wings and eyes lighting up as she spoke, "everyone would be happier."

"That makes sense," I said. "So, what can fairies do for us?"

"We can help you create experiences. Like if you wish to have more fun, we can create more playtime for you in your day. We love seeing you happy and connecting with your inner kid that will always be inside of you, even as you become an adult. We also help protect the earth, especially animals and plants. Of course, we sometimes use a little magic of our own—we may see something you need and find a way to make it show up in your life unexpectedly," Athena said. "The best part is that fairies love to work together with all other mystical and divine beings that come from our magical universe of unconditional love."

"How do I ask the fairies for help?" I stepped closer to Athena.

Athena's face lit up again. "Everyone has fairy guides they can ask for help, even adults. Ask as much as you want—it's so simple! Just remember ABA: it stands for Ask, Believe, and Accept."

"So is that why Teddy left me? Because I didn't believe?" Sadness suddenly filled my throat, just like when I heard my mom had died.

"He didn't leave! He is always with you. He's just waiting for you to be ready to see him again. There is nothing to be afraid of. He really wants to play with you again," Athena said kindly.

My throat felt heavier. "But how do I do that?"

"You simply change your thoughts," she explained. "Those disbelieving thoughts you picked up from your parents and the rest of the world. Your older brother also had a fairy friend he stopped seeing. He convinced you that fairies were only in your imagination." Athena looked at me encouragingly and smiled.

"So—will I see Teddy again?" I looked down at my feet, trying not to cry.

"I know that you will," she promised. "But you need to believe in yourself and trust yourself first. And remember—you can also feel, hear, know, or think about Teddy, too. There are many ways to connect with a fairy being. You just need to start the conversation when you're ready. The rest will follow!" Athena said kindly.

"Hey! When you said that, I felt a spark growing in my heart!" I moved a hand up to my heart. I felt so alive.

"That's a wonderful start, Jackson. Good for you for recognizing a sign. Cally finds it easier to see things, but you feel them. As you both grow in your adventures, your senses will get stronger and more open," Athena explained.

I took a deep breath and nodded.

"Do you want to try something that might help?" she asked.

I nodded again.

"All right, then. Look at the edges around your hand. Now let your eyes blur a little. What do you see?"

43

"It's just a bit fuzzy . . . No, wait, I see a little glow of yellow light," I said. "Oh, no! It's fading! I can't see it anymore." I couldn't believe how disappointed I felt.

"Don't worry, Jackson. Just keep practising. It will get clearer. This is how you can see the energy within and around your hand. But remember—sometimes we are only meant to see certain things for a reason, and at the right time," Athena said encouragingly.

Suddenly, I heard Max barking in the distance. As I looked over, he was bouncing up and down, looking like he was right at home.

"How does Max know what to do?" I asked.

"Well, he's always open. He has a good balance of all the senses because he believes what he's experiencing is real." Athena then waved her hand towards him and said, "Come on, let's see him in action."

I followed the flowers behind Athena's purple sparkle, feeling my sadness melt away with every step.

CHAPTER 9
Cally

As I walked closer to the rest of the group, I saw Jackson trying to catch up to Max. My dog was gleeful, still floating above ground.

I heard Athena laugh as two younger-looking fairies instantly appeared just beside Max. One had blond hair and was wearing a leaf crown and shorts made of leaves. The other fairy was in the shape of a yellow daisy. It was like the fairy was part of the flower itself.

"As you can see, Max already knows his team quite well. He communicates and plays with these two whenever he remembers to. He loves visiting Fairyland because he can float when he's here. Like most pets, he's a pure bundle of unconditional love," Athena explained.

Max and his two fairies started running around the lagoon. We walked after him.

I heard soft music as we approached Max and his fairy team. They were all floating around a willow tree by the pond. The tree was surrounded by gnomes of different sizes making circles around it. They wore bouncy hats and smiled happily at the tree.

Suddenly, I recognized it as the one in the middle of the land—the tree we'd seen earlier when we were flying with the unicorn.

"That looks like fun!" I said, clapping my hands in excitement. "What are they doing?"

"They're activating the Tree of Imagination." Athena smiled.

"Why? What does it do?" I asked her.

"It's a special tree that represents Mother Earth. Through her, it has magical healing powers coming from the earth's ancient energy and wisdom. Come, let's join the dance and see the magic ourselves." Athena danced her way to the tree.

Before either of us could hesitate, we were dancing around the tree with Athena, her flowers, and Max and his fairy team.

I was doing my favourite giraffe dance move while Jackson moved his feet in circles.

"Where is the music coming from?" he called. The music had become so loud that Jackson had to shout over it as we danced.

I listened for a while before I figured it out. "Oh, Jackson! I think it's coming from the tree, the gnomes, the flowers, the earth itself, and even us!"

Jackson got an intense look on his face as he listened with all his attention. Then he jumped back a step.

"Athena, how come I can hear you as thoughts in my head?" he asked.

"Everyone can. We just need to be in the right state to really listen. You humans call it telepathy," she said aloud.

"Can Cally do it, too?" Jackson said.

"Sometimes. But it only works when she's connected to the earth. When she becomes more grounded, it will work more often. All in good time!" I realized that Athena had replied to both of us telepathically.

Then she said aloud, "Don't worry, Cally. You'll remember what you need to do when you need it."

"Will I be able to, as well?" Jackson asked. "I keep worrying that I won't."

"The best way is to enjoy this moment. *This* is what life is all about—be here, in the now," her voice said kindly. "When you focus on something it expands in energy. It's like when you keep having a recurring thought. The more you think it and give it energy, the more likely it will show up in the world."

With every footstep I took, I felt an inner beat that guided me somehow. I wanted to stay in Fairyland forever.

When I looked back to smile at Jackson, he was gone.

"Where's Jackson?" I asked Athena.

"Don't worry, he's okay," Athena said as she slowed down her speed and looked at me with love in her eyes. "He went home, back to Kalamazoo."

"But why? He was so happy here! I could see it in his eyes and in the halo that surrounded him," I said, feeling confused.

"The important thing to know is that he's fine," Athena said gently. "What colours did you notice in his halo while he was dancing?"

"There was a mix of yellow, blue, and purple flickering around him," I said.

"That was his aura—his energy field. The colours show what's happening within someone and can be seen, felt, or just known," Athena explained.

"What do Jackson's yellow, blue, and purple colours mean?" I asked.

"They mean many things, but just now they conveyed that he was feeling happy, safe, and loved," Athena said.

I smiled. Athena's explanations made me feel like what I was experiencing in this moment was real. That I could see auras, too.

Suddenly, I remembered a time that I'd actually seen someone's aura.

A few years ago, my family invited our new neighbour over. When Mom answered the door, I could see a strong yellow colour surrounding the elderly woman. Without thinking, I asked, "Is your favourite colour yellow?"

The lady laughed. "Why would you say that?"

"I can see a yellow glow around you," I said softly.

The lady was speechless, and my mom's face went red with embarrassment. Mom quickly looked at me then back at our new neighbour. It took a few moments, but finally they both just laughed, and my mom said, "Oh, the crazy things wee ones say."

"I'm Miss Adams," she said to me when she stopped chuckling. "And yes, I do like yellow."

She was nice about it, but after that day, Miss Adams stayed away from me. When I walked Max by her house or played outside with Jackson, Miss Adams walked quickly past me while crossing her heart and muttering something to herself. At those times, her yellow glow turned grey. I think she found me weird.

I couldn't get the image of Miss Adams's grey aura out of my head as I tried to smile at Athena.

I started feeling dizzy and closed my eyes as Athena was saying, "You must always stay in the moment to stay in . . ."

Her voice faded away. All I could see was Miss Adams's grey glow.

CHAPTER 10
Jackson

I was sliding. Down . . . down . . . down . . . My arms and legs were shaking. Even my eyes felt fuzzy. Leaves floated below me as I passed by tunnels all around me. Where was I? Where were Cally and Max? The last thing I could remember was dancing around the Tree of Imagination with them.

I felt better for a moment when a bright yellow spark lit up in front of me, but then it disappeared.

"What's happening?!" I shouted as loud as I could. I tried to steady myself as the tree branches moved me past the different exits on the Green Man's slide. Where was it taking me?

I thought about Cally and wished she was with me. Was she safe?

"Everything is all right." I felt the slide start to vibrate with the Green Man's voice.

"Where are you taking me? I want to go back to Fairyland!" I shouted at the Green Man.

The slide became less steep and more leaves gathered below me, slowing me down.

"It's time for you to go home, Jackson," his deep voice echoed around me.

"Why is this happening?! I don't *want* to go home yet!" I yelled back.

"But you must. And why do you think that is?" the Green Man asked calmly.

"I'm not sure. I was dancing around the tree . . . and then I was afraid I'd forget how I felt in Fairyland. Everything went fuzzy. That's all I remember."

"You must let go of the fear, Jackson. That is your task. You need to go home to practise."

"But I want to find Teddy!" I felt a heaviness in my stomach.

"Remember what Athena said, Teddy is always with you."

"But I want to *see* him!"

Just as I was about to complain about how unfair this was, a rainbow light shaped like a snow angel appeared in front of me. Then the light turned into a butterfly shape, and my mom's face was there. She was smiling at me. I reached out to touch her, but she disappeared into a tunnel.

"Come back, Mom!" I looked behind me for her face, the face I hadn't seen in six years. Was she okay? Was she safe? Happy?

"She will visit you and your dad again soon," the Green Man promised softly.

I blinked hard as I fixed my glasses.

Before I could ask more, the slide opened up to a bright blue sky. I found myself standing in the park without knowing how I'd arrived there.

As the tree slide closed, I heard a loud sneeze.

CHAPTER 11
Cally

"Bless you."

I could hear Jackson's voice as I covered my mouth. Our eyes met as I ran over to him.

When he stood up, I gave him a big hug.

"Do you have to do that, Cally?" he asked, squirming his way out of my grip.

"I'm so glad you're okay!" I said as I let go of him. He smiled a bit.

"I was worried about you when I didn't see you on the Green Man's slide." He wrinkled his nose. "I think I saw my mom, though."

"What? But *how*?" I knew how much he missed her.

"When I was on the slide, she appeared for an instant out of the form of a rainbow butterfly. But then suddenly I was here." He paused and asked, "Wait—how *did* you get back here?"

"I'm not sure—I just remember having the best time. Then a weird memory about Miss Adams changed everything. I think Athena was trying to help me, but she faded out," I said.

"Well, we have to get back there! How do we go back?" Jackson asked.

"I don't know," I said, missing Fairyland already. "It's too bad Max can't talk. Maybe he could tell us."

"Maybe Max can tell us in his own way," Jackson said slowly.

I clapped my hands together. "I can't believe you just said that, Jackson! Who *are* you? Where is my sceptical, logical friend?" I hugged him again, and this time he didn't squirm.

"You're right! It's worth a shot," I said, following Jackson towards home.

***

My elbow started to tickle on the way home. It reminded me of Celtic Thunder, but when I brushed it lightly with my hand, it stopped.

When I walked into my house, I looked at the clock in the living room. It was only five o'clock. Not even dinnertime yet!

I couldn't believe that was the time. We'd only been in Fairyland for an hour? It seemed impossible.

It made me wonder, was time different in Fairyland?

"Yes," a small voice whispered in my thoughts.

I was about to reply when my mom yelled, "Dinner's ready!"

I walked into the kitchen and noticed Max sitting on his daybed by the dinner table.

How had he arrived back home so quickly?

Just then I heard the loud sound of a cow going, "Moo, moo, moooooo . . ." It was my little brother, Wes, racing in front of me, pushing one of his beanbag toys along the floor.

It felt like forever since I'd seen him. I couldn't resist my brother's cute dimples and messy blond hair. Kneeling down, I joined in the fun with my best cow sounds.

As we were playing, he pointed at my mom. Green sparks floated around her head as she hummed and set out the food on the dinner table.

"Can you see fairies, too?" I asked, looking back at him in excitement.

He just giggled and continued to play with his cow.

Oh, my goodness—this must run in the family!

But when I looked up at Mom again, the sparks were gone.

***

After dinner, Max followed me up to my room. As soon as I sat on my bed, I asked him, "How do we get back to Fairyland? And how did you get home so quickly?"

But he just looked at me with his big brown eyes and put his paw on my leg. When he closed his eyes and started snoring, I gave up.

Frustrated, I went back downstairs for some juice.

When I was halfway down the stairs, I heard my mom on the phone, saying, "I'm so tired of being alone, Ruth. It's so hard."

I couldn't help myself. All of the energy I had spent trying to make my mom happy, missing my dad, and keeping my emotions bottled up finally spilled over. I sprinted into the kitchen and yelled, "Don't you ever think I feel alone, too? You barely have time for me anymore! We never have fun like we used to!"

Her face was unreadable. "I've got to go, Ruth," she said as she hung up. "Cally, you know better than to listen to my calls!" Her eyes got bigger as she stepped closer to me. "I have a lot going on, Cally—it's not easy raising you and Wes alone. I'm knackered and just getting by," she said as she dropped heavily into a kitchen chair. "As much as things weren't always good in our marriage, I miss your father."

"Well, I miss him, too," I said, walking away. I clenched my hands until my knuckles started turning red.

"And you're not alone, Mom! You have Wes, and Max, and me!" I yelled as I ran back to my room.

I tried to shake out the anger like Skye showed me, but it didn't go anywhere.

I punched my pillow and then collapsed onto my bed. Tears formed in my eyes. Then I noticed a purple spark blink in front of me. I knew Athena was near, but I was too tired to try to reach her. I just snuggled up to Max and drifted off.

***

My eyes were puffy the next day, so I left for school early to avoid my mom.

I didn't see Jackson all day, but after school we walked home together.

"Did you try talking to Max?" Jackson asked.

"I tried. All he did was look at me and put his paw on my leg." I started walking ahead.

"But I did figure out that Wes can see fairies, too!" I said, smiling.

"That's amazing, Cally!" Jackson kicked some stones off the sidewalk. His face was intense, thoughtful.

He took a deep breath and said, "Something has been following me lately."

"What! What do you mean?" I asked.

"I don't know, exactly. I can't see it, but I can feel it." He looked down. "Since I've been back from Fairyland, I feel more . . . It's hard to explain . . ."

"What do you feel right now? Is it here with us?" Light, warm shivers cascaded down my shoulders.

"Wow, did you just feel that?" Jackson stopped dead in his tracks.

"Yes, it was quick, but I definitely felt something." Our eyes met. "What was it?"

"I know this is going to sound crazy, but I think it's someone trying to get our attention. Lately, I've been feeling like I need to look up into the sky. Whenever I do, I see shapes in the clouds. The other day I got tingles, and there were fluffy wing-shaped clouds in the sky." Jackson smiled at the memory.

"Whoa, that's so cool!" I yelled.

"I thought I saw something a few minutes ago when we were leaving school, but I didn't want to sound weird." Jackson wrinkled his nose.

"I think we're way past weird after our last adventure." I giggled out loud. "How do these cloud wings make you feel?" I asked.

"Safe and loved. Like they're here to help us in some way. Like somehow we asked for help." Jackson paused. "Hey! Look up, Cally!" He pointed to the baby blue sky.

"Oh, my gosh!" I yelled. Something moved between the swirls of smooth white clouds. When I looked closer, I saw soft, flowing white wings.

"Can you see them, Cally?" Jackson's voice echoed in my ear.

"Angels!" I felt my heart skip a beat.

CHAPTER 12
Jackson

I kept tossing and turning. I couldn't fall asleep. When I finally looked at my alarm clock, it read 11:11 p.m.

I couldn't stop thinking about the angel clouds. I got up from my warm bed to peer out my window. The dark ashy sky was calm, not a cloud in sight.

When I was getting back into bed, I accidentally knocked my glass of water off the nightstand.

I tried to reach for it before it hit the ground, but it fell hard and fast against the grey carpet with a loud THUMP.

When I looked at the water on the floor, I saw a rainbow butterfly. As I reached for it, the light turned on in the hallway, and the butterfly disappeared.

"Jackson, is everything okay in there?" my dad's sleepy voice bellowed, he was always a light sleeper.

I looked back down at the water and saw the shape of a smile.

"Everything's fine," I said back. "I'm sorry, I . . ." My dad was already at my door, wearing his old red-and-white-plaid flannel pajamas.

"Bean, are you sure everything is okay?" He'd called me Bean ever since I was obsessed with saying "Jelly Beans!" over and over when I was little.

"I'm sorry if I woke you." I sat up.

He sat on my bed, wiped his tired eyes, and then picked up the glass from the floor. "What's keeping you up?"

"Dad, do you believe in angels?" I noticed some white hairs peeking out from his rich brown beard.

He sighed. "I used to. When I was a kid and went to church, there were many angels mentioned in the Bible. In those stories they showed themselves sometimes when people asked for help. I believed the stories for a long time."

"Why don't you believe in them now?" I asked.

"After your mom died, I just couldn't anymore." His brown eyes grew sad.

I hesitated for a second and then leaned in for a hug. His hugs weren't as tight as they used to be.

"Thanks, Bean." He lightly squeezed my hand as he let go. "I love you more than anything. Now it's time to go to sleep."

I laid back in my bed. "Sweet dreams, Dad."

"Sweet dreams, Bean." Right before he left, he turned and asked, "Hey. Why are you interested in angels all of a sudden?"

"I have this feeling they might be contacting me. Does that sound crazy?"

A slight gleam of hope returned to his eyes. "Not at all," he said as he stepped into the hallway.

***

The next morning I opened my front door when Cally was halfway down the sidewalk on my street. She waved when she saw me.

"I had a feeling you were coming." I skipped towards her.

I stopped and blushed. What was I doing?

"You seem happy!" Cally giggled.

I felt my face turning red, so I adjusted my glasses.

"I really want to go back to Fairyland! I'm here to make a plan. Let's figure this out!"

"Me, too, Cally, but first I need to tell you what I found out this morning."

"What is it, Jackson?" Cally clapped her hands.

"I just had the feeling suddenly that I should look for more information about angels in my mom's old book collection. I read for ages. There are so many things that make sense to me now!"

We sat down on a bench in the front yard.

"What? Tell me!"

"It was really cool . . . When I stood in front of the bookshelf, my eyes and fingers were guided to a book called *Angels Among Us*."

"And?" Cally was so excited she could barely sit on the bench.

"It was like the book was there waiting for me for this exact time. It was weird but extremely cool . . . The book says that there are many kinds of angels, and seeing double digits and wings is a sign they're communicating with me."

"Awesome!" She smiled back, hardly sitting still. "So what kinds of angels are trying to help us?"

"Well, it turns out that everyone has guardian angels by their sides. They come into our lives with us to help with whatever we need." I smiled.

"That makes sense," she said. "They're like fairies that way. I wonder if they all work together to help us?"

"I betcha they do." I stood up and paused.

"I just felt shivers. I think there are angels here right now!" Cally stood up next to me.

"I feel like it's a 'he'," I said, and she look amazed.

Cally started to pace back and forth. "Okay then, I guess we should ask him some questions . . . hmm . . . What's his name?"

"Michael." I was surprised at how quickly the words came out of my mouth. "He tells me that we shouldn't be afraid. He's been trying to talk to us for some time." How did I know what to say? Nothing like this had ever happened to me before.

"Why can't we see him?" Cally asked.

I zoned out for a second, trying to feel Michael's presence.

Cally started to tap her foot on the ground.

"Hello? Are you listening to me?" Cally finally asked.

"I'm sorry, I can't hear him anymore," I said.

"Why? What were you thinking about?" she asked and looked down at the ground.

"I heard something, but then I worried I was talking crazy, that I shouldn't be talking about something neither of us can see," I said.

"But we *have* seen him. In the clouds!"

The air between us felt heavy.

"You have to stop doing this, Jackson! Your worries made you leave Fairyland. Now they're going to drive the angels away!"

"I don't want to drive them away!" I was mad at myself, but I was even more mad at her. "It's not easy for me to let go of my worries, Cally! You make it look so simple."

Cally stood there quietly as I tried to calm down.

"But you're right, Cally. I was worried about forgetting the feeling of Fairyland. That it . . . or I . . ."

"You let your thoughts take you out of the present moment," Cally said softly.

"But how do I stop that from happening?" I wondered.

"I don't know," she admitted. "That's what happened to me, too." She looked sad.

"So then, how do we get back?" I asked her.

"I'm not sure," she said with doubt in her eyes. "I thought we could make a plan, but . . . I just don't feel like it anymore. I'm going home."

"Cally, wait!"

But she was already gone.

CHAPTER 13
Cally

I ran until I passed the dog park. When I got around the corner and onto my block, I slowed down. There was a breeze, and the swaying tree branches caught my eye. I wished they could move like the ones in Fairyland, but they just stood there being normal trees. How were we ever going to get back there—especially with Jackson's fears ruining everything?

When I passed my neighbour's house I saw his Siamese cat, Sedona, on an old wicker chair by the porch. She was so beautiful. Her blue eyes looked like clear water, and her grey-and-white coat made her look wise.

She had to be at least sixteen years old. I remembered Mr. Talisman inviting our family to her birthday last fall. She had been living in the house beside me for as long as I could remember.

I realized that I'd never once seen Sedona outside. As far as I knew, her owner, Mr. Talisman, never let her out.

"Here, Sedona, here!" I called as I walked towards their driveway.

She jumped off the chair and looked up at the light blue sky.

It was another beautiful, clear September day.

As I looked up, I saw a soft thick cloud appear out of nowhere. The cloud became fluffier as I focused on it. After a few seconds, the cloud turned into a winged angel shape surrounded by an aura that was a blue darker than the sky itself.

I looked back at Sedona. "Did you know that was going to happen?" I said aloud to her, as she circled me with her thick grey tail.

Looking at Sedona, I noticed her small lips curve into a mischievous smile—like something out of a storybook. Then I looked up at the sky again, and it was completely clear. The cloud was gone.

The cat's eyes seemed excited.

"Okay, it's time for you to go back inside." I reached down to grab her.

She was too quick. Before I could catch her, she was on the sidewalk that led to the park.

"You gave me a reason to leave the house."

The low voice was coming from inside my head! Then I noticed Sedona looking back at me.

"How are you doing that, Sedona? How are you talking to me in my head?" I asked aloud, walking towards her.

"The energy centres around your ears are finally open, Cally," I heard her voice explain. "We call them your ear chakras."

"Can you enter people's thoughts whenever you want?" I asked her, this time from inside my head.

"Yes. But I rarely do. I figured it was time for you to hear me," Sedona said inside my head.

"Why? And where are we going?" I asked, hurrying to catch up to her.

Sedona looked back at me again and fluffed up her tail towards the sky. "We're going to meet someone," she answered.

I was so busy watching her that I tripped over the uneven sidewalk and landed in a small puddle on the road. When I lifted my red sneaker out to shake the water off, orange-and-blue sparks flashed before me.

CHAPTER 14
Jackson

When Cally left I went home again to look at my mom's books some more. But after just twenty minutes, I felt a light pink energy come over me, and I knew she was on her way back.

I looked out my living room window and there she was. She seemed really out of it.

I ran to the front door and yelled, "Cally!"

She just kept walking, so I ran down the street to catch up with her. I realized she was following Sedona, Mr. Talisman's cat.

The cat's tail shot up instantly when I reached Cally. Sedona started running. Cally and I followed.

"Why are we following Sedona? Where is she going?" I shouted, trying to get Cally's attention.

"She told me that we're going to meet someone," Cally said. "And just a minute ago as I was following her, I saw a glimpse of my water fairies!"

"I don't think we can trust her!" I grabbed Cally's arm, trying to stop her.

"Let go of me, Jackson!" Cally pulled away from my grip. "I'm done with letting your fears hold me back. Just because you don't trust her doesn't mean you're right! I don't have to listen to you. You're always holding me back, and I'm tired of it!" She stomped her feet like a child.

She'd never talked to me like this.

"But Cally, you're always running around so distracted and all over the place. I have to look out for you. If I didn't, then who would?"

"Stop *worrying*, Jackson! Just accept that I'm one area of your life you can't control. I don't fit in a box!"

"Cally, I . . ." But I couldn't finish. Tears started to fall down my cheek. I stopped, feeling numb. I couldn't move. She sounded like my older brother when he got impatient with me.

I stood there alone on the sidewalk.

Then Sedona sauntered towards me and rubbed against my leg. She was surprisingly warm, comforting.

I started to wipe my tears, and Cally turned back to me. Sedona patted my shoe with her smoky-grey paw. I wanted to pick her up.

I hesitated, and she lightly pawed my shoe again.

As I picked her up, her tail wrapped around my index finger. My tears began to fade when she started purring.

"You see, she's not that bad," Cally said, patting Sedona's head.

"I never thought in a million years that this cat would make me feel better. She always seemed so protective of Mr. Talisman." I patted down her fur.

"She says that's only because she agreed to watch over him. It was a pact she made with him before she came here."

"How did she tell you that, Cally?" I said, wiping the last of my tears away.

"She's telepathic, I think," Cally said, with her brown eyes growing bigger. "So, are you ready to come and see where she's leading us?"

I set Sedona down and for a quick second I saw a flash of yellow light. I was definitely curious.

"Okay," I said with a slight smile. "Let's go."

CHAPTER 15
Cally

Sedona led us back to the park where we had first entered Fairyland.

As we passed the tree where the Green Man resided, I looked at it carefully. But the tree just looked like any other old tree.

Why couldn't I see him this time?

Sedona responded quickly by saying, "You can only see him when you're open and present—like you were in Fairyland."

"How do you know what happened when we were in Fairyland?" Jackson asked Sedona.

"I just had a feeling something was going on when Cally smiled at me today." Sedona flashed her mischievous grin. "Her energy was so different—more magical. I figured you went on an adventure. Besides, it's not the first time Cally's been there. When she was younger, you and I went there with her all the time," Sedona said in our minds.

"I don't remember that," I said aloud.

"This is getting really confusing, talking in our heads half the time," Jackson said aloud to both of us.

"Well, I'm just glad you're finally listening. We've talked before, Jackson—many times, when you were hanging out with Cally in the backyard. Don't you remember seeing me on my window ledge?" Sedona asked.

The cat laughed a little as Jackson and I looked at each other, even more confused.

"It doesn't really matter whether we remember what happened then," I insisted. "What matters now is getting back to Fairyland. Sedona, do you know how?" I said this out loud, as Jackson just stood there staring at her with big eyes.

"Just remember, we're all connected," she said. Then Sedona disappeared into the bushes.

I started to follow her. "Hey! You didn't answer my question!"

I was about to climb into the bushes when a blue fog formed in front of us. It was exactly the colour I'd seen in the sky a few minutes earlier.

"Are you seeing what I'm seeing?" I looked at Jackson.

Jackson nodded and pushed his glasses up higher on his nose, squinting at the fog.

The more I focused on the fog, the brighter and more vivid the colour got.

Jackson looked at me, and I could tell he felt calmer. I had a familiar feeling that we were supposed to be there in that moment. Like it was planned somehow.

"It's like we've been here before!" Jackson took the words right out of my mouth.

I felt a warmth in my stomach and put my hands on it for a second. Jackson looked at me again and I saw his hands were on his stomach, too.

In my head I heard him ask, "*Have* we done this before?"

I laughed and said back with my mind, "I was just wondering that."

CHAPTER 16
Jackson

The fog lifted, and suddenly two cobalt-blue wings emerged from the bushes. A figure with long dark hair appeared between the wings. He was at least seven feet tall.

"Wow!" I said out loud.

His eyes were like nothing I'd ever seen before. They were vivid and intense, shining a strong indigo blue. And when he looked at me, I felt loved instantly.

He carried with him a round bronze shield that was shining with white-and-yellow light. Looking at the shield and the light made my body feel stronger. I stood taller.

"Cool shield!" Cally said to him.

The angel simply nodded.

Then I noticed he was holding a sword, but it wasn't like any sword I'd seen before, let alone imagined. It was glistening with transparent golden light. There were white wings and a gold snake figure wrapped around its handle. I couldn't take my eyes off of it. Something about the way it shone was so majestic.

"It's you—Michael!" I gasped, staring into his piercing eyes.

"Yes," he said. "Hello again, Jackson and Cally. I am Michael. And I know both of you very well." Even his voice had a strong presence. His tone was loving, but so powerful.

I was in awe of his words. Not knowing what to say, I stood in silence beside Cally.

"What kind of angel are you?" Cally piped in.

"He's an archangel!" I answered without thinking. "I read about archangels in that book I was telling you about. It said that they watch over our guardian angels. And they can even be with more than one person at any time." I was surprised the words came out of my mouth so quickly. I didn't even remember reading that.

"Jackson is right. Each of you has your own unique energy and vibration, so we can find you wherever you are, whenever you ask." The angel's smile grew even bigger.

"So archangels go anywhere they're needed?" Cally asked.

"Yes!" Michael laughed with joy. His laugh was so infectious that Cally and I had to laugh, too.

Cally smiled and asked, "Where did Sedona go? Did she summon you?"

"Yes. We've known each other for a long time." Michael smiled again. "She did what she needed to do today, so she's gone back home."

"So you work with all kinds of beings? Like on the way here I saw my water fairies. They seemed like they were telling me to keep going." Cally smiled. "Was that because of you?"

"That's right. Many beings help along the way."

Then Archangel Michael's shield lit up again.

The shield's glow went right through me. I felt like I knew Michael. His presence gave me such comfort and joy. My whole body felt happier than I could ever remember.

Michael said, "Jackson, I feel the same way about you."

Cally stepped closer to me. I knew that she felt the same way about Michael. I just knew.

"Michael, can you help us get back to Fairyland?" Cally asked.

Michael pulled two gleaming swords from under his wings and handed one to each of us.

"Yes. You are ready now. I brought both of you a gift of love so you can get back there, to Fairyland."

Cally's sword lit up with soft purple sparkles. Around the handle there were transcendent fairy wings, and magic white light surrounded the sword. The ground started vibrating, and I stepped back as I felt an energetic power surge through her heart when she picked up the sword.

Michael turned to me with the other sword lighting up in his strong hands. It glowed with a dark blue, yellow, and green swirling light. "For you, Jackson," he said.

My hands started to tingle when he placed it in my palms.

Energy from the sword cascaded through my fingertips and up my arms to my heart. It was so powerful it was almost scary, but when I noticed the handle was surrounded by outlines of wings like Michael's, I felt strong and safe.

As I raised the sword up, the power expanded into my heart.

I was about to thank Michael when he started to speak again.

"This sword is a gift from me to you. Just like my sword, yours will cut away any fear that interrupts your adventures. After all, this is only the beginning of many adventures to come. Just remember, these journeys are gifts to you and to the world," Michael said. "So whenever you fear, your sword will appear."

"Wow! Thank you, Michael," Cally said with the biggest smile I'd ever seen.

I hugged Michael without even realizing what I was doing. When I hugged him I felt complete, and my heart was lighter.

Then Cally joined in, and Michael's wings embraced us both for a long time.

"Can I ask you something, Michael?" I said when we stepped back.

"Of course," he replied.

"Is my mom okay?" A lump formed in my throat as soon as I said the words.

He looked at me kindly. "Yes, Jackson," he said gently. "She is more than okay—she's at peace, in perfect harmony. And just like the angels, fairies, and butterflies, she is always with you no matter what."

The lump in my throat disappeared. "Thank you, Michael!" I felt like I'd just set down a thousand-pound boulder that I'd been carrying for years.

"You're welcome. I am here to make your life easier, just like all your divine helpers. You are never alone. You need never struggle unaided. Now let's get you two back to Fairyland. The fairies are waiting," Michael said with a beautiful glimmer in his cobalt-blue eyes.

"And remember—if you notice Fairyland beginning to fade away again, just use your swords. All you have to do is say, 'I choose love right now.' With these words, even if you can't see, hear, or feel me, I will take away your fear. Don't forget—you can always call on me. I'll be there right away. You can always trust that I'm there, helping you. It's time to try it now. Ready? One . . . two . . . three . . ."

CHAPTER 17
Cally

"I choose love right now!" I heard Jackson shout, as Michael's voice faded away.

I opened my eyes and started dancing. "We're back!" I yelled, noticing my sword shrink into my jacket pocket.

We'd arrived at the maple tree near the elf. "Indeed you are, Cally. We're so glad to see you again!" he said.

Then the elf grabbed my hands and started tapping his feet into square patterns. I was about to repeat his steps when I saw Jackson sitting near one of the tall tree houses.

He looked at me with sadness in his eyes. "I miss Michael already."

"Jackson, don't you remember what he *just* told us? He's always with us no matter what. You need to believe that!" I felt impatient already. Was he going to ruin another moment in Fairyland? Then I felt terrible—he looked so sad. "Here," I said, reaching out my hand.

He took it, and I helped him off the ground.

"Thanks, Cally. You always know how to make me feel better," he said, starting to smile.

The elf walked over to us, saying, "I just knew Archangel Michael would help you get back here. We've been waiting for you!"

"It's so cool that you are all connected." Jackson smiled at the elf.

Suddenly, the fairies' lights began gathering around me. I could see a yellow light surround Jackson. Then I saw Athena's purple glow.

As I focused on the light, Athena flew towards us. I gave her a big hug. Jackson joined in, too.

When her sparkles completely surrounded the three of us, she said, "I never left you two. I've always been with you."

"Then how come I've only seen you once in the last few days?" I questioned.

"Cally, I never left your side." Athena's eyes sparkled as she talked.

"But I don't understand!"

With those words, Fairyland started to fade away again.

I knew just what to do, and my heart sang it like a song: "I choose love right now. I choose love right now. I choose love right now! I am always connected to love."

The fading subsided, and Athena's face reappeared in front of me.

"I'm sorry," I said, reaching out to her. "It's not that I don't believe you. I just missed you so much!" Tears were forming in my eyes.

"I know. And I know sometimes you feel different from everyone else. But those are just illusions. Pay no attention to them. For there are so many sparks of love that surround you always." Athena smiled at me kindly.

Her words reminded me of how I'd felt a few days earlier—just before I saw the spark in my room. But now I knew: I wasn't alone after all! I'm just as unique as everyone else in the world, and we are all connected through our different sparks, our hearts.

I smiled at Athena with tears streaming down my cheeks.

She took our hands, saying, "It's time to go to the Tree of Imagination." Athena called the unicorn over, grabbed my hand, and we all jumped on its back together.

In a moment we were flying.

CHAPTER 18
Jackson

I'd barely had time to realize we were back in Fairyland before we landed in front of the Tree of Imagination. Everything was happening so fast! But I wasn't scared anymore.

As we dismounted from the unicorn, all of us started walking over to the tree.

Warm shivers crept up my leg. When I looked down, I saw Sedona patting my white sneaker with her velvety grey paw.

"I'm so glad to see you!" I told her.

She smiled when I picked her up, patting her silky fur. She was purring. In that moment, I knew this wasn't our first time together in Fairyland.

"I told you so," I heard her voice laugh in my head.

I laughed aloud. After a few minutes, I placed Sedona back on the ground.

"Come on, Jackson! It's time to celebrate. You're back!" Athena took Cally and me by the hand, leading us closer to the tree.

As we approached, I saw lights, fairies, elves, animals, and plants of all kinds dancing around the tree. Magic flew in a sparkly cloud, surrounding the tree. Colours danced in the wind.

Sedona joined us, and we all danced together with these mystical creatures.

Soon wings appeared in the sky, and I knew he was there, too, Archangel Michael. I felt the shrunken sword warm up in my pocket.

A song floated out of the tree itself, adding rhythm to everyone's steps. I felt a gentle harmony as the song filled the spaces between our steps:

> *We are all a part of this imagi-*
> *nation tree*
> *One and the same*
> *We choose to believe in its*
> *power, its place*
> *We circle the tree to tap into the*
> *wisdom of love*
> *So set your intention*
> *So you might experience*

*its magic
And discover what you
really believe
Feel it in your heart
See it in a picture
Hear it in your mind
Know it to be true
As we are all a part of this
imagination tree.*

The lyrics sang to me, as if somehow I'd always known them.

As I focused on the tree, I noticed a bright yellow light glowing from it. When the light flew towards the fairy pond, I left the circle to sprint after it. But as soon I got closer, it disappeared into the grass below.

I knelt down on the ground, searching the grass. "Where'd you go?" I asked aloud.

A slight hum came from below my fingertips, but I couldn't see anything.

Then a voice filled my heart—not my ears, not my mind, but my *heart*, saying, "It's been way too long."

"Is that you, Teddy?!" I said excitedly, without understanding how I knew it was him.

"Stick around and you might find out," he said with a laugh. His voice got louder and happier with each word.

The yellow light I'd followed emerged from the ground, expanding as it landed on a white cactus in front of me.

When I reached out to touch it, it flew away again. I chuckled, following him. This was the same game of chase I'd played with Teddy when I was little!

The memory came back to me as I ran after the warm glow. I was about four years old, playing in my backyard. I was running around, laughing, jumping up and down. Between my laughter and excitement, I could see someone playing with me . . . It was Teddy, the fairy I was seeing now!

Then the bright yellow light grew into a small figure that landed on the ground beside me. His dark yellow wings were made of leaves, and he had a round belly. His white beard moved as he tugged his hat of branches down on his head. His eyes glistened with brown-and-green light.

"Teddy!" I hugged him. "Where have you been?" Teddy glanced at me with his bright green eyes.

"I've been here," Teddy's soft voice echoed in my ear, and I felt and saw a warm yellow spark travel into my heart. It was like I was remembering what it felt like to be my four-year-old self again. "I'm always with you. I promise."

I remembered that Athena had also promised me this. Why was it so hard to remember?

"I'm proud of you—you've learned to trust your inner child again," Teddy said.

"Where was my inner child all this time?" I looked at Teddy.

"When you followed Cally here the first time, your inner kid wanted you to do it. Believe it or not, that loving curiosity you see in her is also in *you*. That's your inner kid!" He smiled.

"I see that curiosity in you—you must bring it out in me, too," I replied, smiling back at him.

"It's what I'm here for," Teddy said.

"Thank you," I said. "I'll remember that."

We walked together towards the group.

As we were walking, the soft rainbow butterfly I'd seen when my mom passed away appeared. It was the same one I'd seen on the slide and on the floor of my room. The butterfly landed on Teddy's hand, and my heart filled with peace.

CHAPTER 19
Cally

I clapped my hands as I noticed Jackson with a yellow spark by the tree.

Then I looked at Athena and saw that Sedona had joined the dancing around the tree.

"How did Sedona get here?" I asked Athena.

"There are many ways to get in and out of Fairyland," Athena explained with a smile on her face. "The Tree of Imagination represents Mother Earth, also known as Lady Gaia. She holds the wisdom of the earth. And like all things in the physical world, this tree reflects everything we need to know right now."

The song from the tree got louder. I felt light tickles on my arm.

"Celtic Thunder!" I picked the little green fairy up in my palm and kissed his forehead.

"Don't make me blush!" He giggled.

"Was that you on my arm when I was walking home after we left Fairyland?" I asked. "Oh, sorry! I mean, hello! It's wonderful to see you again."

"I think you already know the answer to that."

Celtic Thunder hopped off my hand, blowing me a kiss that sent mini green hearts spraying everywhere.

Then, as the song around us quieted, I saw Sandy's and Skye's sparkles. Athena said to me, "Sometimes, we only see things that we want to see. But if we change our perspectives and open up to the magic of life, we can see that there really is no separation between Fairyland and real life. It's simply what you choose to see and believe."

"I'm so glad that I listened to my heart and followed your spark in my bedroom that day. I felt alone before, but now I can remember this whenever I feel lonely. Thank you, Athena!" I said as I smiled.

"I'm so happy that you came to visit! I've enjoyed being with you. Remember—I'll be in your heart always," she said back.

In that instant, Athena shrank into a purple spark that flew up into the sky before travelling down into my heart.

My aura expanded into an enormous purple glow all around me.

***

The purple glow was still vibrating when I opened my eyes. I was at home lying in my bed. As soon as I sat up, Athena appeared beside me. She smiled kindly, pointing towards my bedroom door.

I saw a green spark light up beside her and vanish through the door. I ran after the spark into the living room, where my mom was folding her favourite Irish flag blanket. Before I reached her, the spark disappeared.

"Lass, come here to me," my mom said, holding out her arms. "I miss having fun with you. Can we try to do something together every week, just you and me?"

I nodded, and she scooped me up in her arms like she did when I was a kid.

"*Oh, Cally girl, the fairies are here*," a familiar voice sang in my ear.

All of sudden, the song "Ireland's Call" started playing from Mom's iPhone.

"That's weird—what a coincidence," she said as she looked at me.

"I haven't heard this song since I was pregnant with you when I lived in Dublin! It was by my favourite band," she said. "This may sound silly, but I always felt a green light around me when I listened to their music. It made me feel grand."

"That's amazing!" I couldn't believe it—she was connected to the fairies, too.

Before I could say anything else, she turned up the song and grabbed my hands. We danced joyfully around the living room. Soon Athena and the green spark were dancing with us.

"Mom, what was the name of the band?" I asked, as we giggled through our dance.

She smiled. "Celtic Thunder, my lass."

Somehow I wasn't surprised by this after everything that had happened.

"I want to take you somewhere later, Mom. Will you come?"

"Anywhere with you, my lass," she said with tears in her eyes.

I knew it was true by the joy and warmth filling my heart.

END

About the Author

DeAnna Kweens lives in Calgary, Alberta with her fairies, angels and unicorns. When DeAnna was a child, she discovered another world beyond what we could see and imagine. She embraces this magical world everyday, and encourages children and adults to discover this magic for themselves.

Visit her at deannakweensauthor.com or @deannakweensauthor on Instagram, TikTok and Facebook.

Printed in Canada